First published 2017
by Bloomsbury Publishing Plc
50 Bedford Square, London WC1B 3DP
www.bloomsbury.com

Bloomsbury is a registered trademark of Bloomsbury Publishing Plc
Copyright © 2017 Bloomsbury Publishing Plc
Text copyright © Fatima Sharfeddine 2017
Illustration copyright © Rasha Munib Al-Hakim 2017

ISBN 978-1-4088-8740-0

A CIP catalogue for this book is available from the British Library.

Printed in China by Leo Paper Products, Heshan, Guangdong

1 3 5 7 9 10 8 6 4 2

BLOOMSBURY
CHILDREN'S
BOOKS

Mimi in Paris

Written by Fatima Sharfeddine
Illustrated by Rasha Munib Al-Hakim

Mimi is on her way to Paris with her family.

The plane journey is long, but Mimi is happy. She listens to music and looks at photos of the French city in her book.

Mimi asks a painter to draw a caricature of her.
She laughs when she sees the size of her long, curly hair!

Later on, Mimi and her family see a group of young people playing music. Crowds gather around to listen and to throw coins into a hat.

They go for a walk in a park and Mimi's mum tells her to close her eyes.

She holds her mum's hand as she leads her to...

She uses her camera to take photos of everything around her, like the historical churches and the cobbled streets.

In a pretty square, there are people selling books, toys and sweets. Mimi and her brother watch some children performing acrobatics. "Don't wander too far from us," says her mum.

...the Eiffel Tower!

It looks high enough
to touch the sky.
They climb up the tower
and look down over the city.

"Paris is so big, Mum!"
Mimi says.

Later, Mimi and her family stop to rest in a café. Lunch is some tasty sandwiches.

"Bread and cheese are very yummy here!" says Mimi.

After she's finished her food, Mimi asks if she can
go to feed the pigeons some breadcrumbs.
Her mum agrees, but reminds her,
"Don't wander too far
away from us."

Birds gather around Mimi as she starts throwing breadcrumbs. They peck at the bread and fly away. Mimi laughs and runs around after them. She keeps running around and around, until...

...she can't see the café anymore!

"Mum, Dad!" she screams, but there is no answer. She runs around in circles, not knowing what to do.

Mimi starts crying.

How will her parents find her? She feels very small and alone.

Suddenly, Mimi remembers that she has a card in her pocket from the hotel where her family are staying.

But how will she get there?

Luckily, a policewoman sees Mimi.
She asks her in French,
"Why are you crying?"

Mimi can't speak French,
but she passes her the hotel card.

The policewoman smiles
at Mimi and says, "Come with me."

When Mimi arrives at the hotel, her family all run towards her.

"We're so glad that you're okay," her mum says.

"I'm so sorry, Mum and Dad," says Mimi. "I was really scared."

"Well, you did very well telling the policewoman what was wrong," says her dad.

"I promise not to wander too far away next time," says Mimi.

"I won't be chasing pigeons
for a while, either."
Mimi thinks to herself.
"But I can't wait to tell my friends
all about my **adventures in Paris!**"